NEW   S

CHILDHOOD FEARS
AND ANXIETIES

NIGHTTIME FEARS

CHILDHOOD FEARS AND ANXIETIES

CHILDHOOD FEARS
AND ANXIETIES

NIGHTTIME
FEARS

H.W. POOLE

SERIES CONSULTANT
ANNE S. WALTERS, Ph.D.

Emma Pendleton Bradley Hospital

Warren Alpert Medical School of
Brown University

MASON CREST

Mason Crest
450 Parkway Drive, Suite D
Broomall, PA 19008
www.masoncrest.com

MTM Publishing, Inc.
435 West 23rd Street, #8C
New York, NY 10011
www.mtmpublishing.com

President: Valerie Tomaselli
Vice President, Book Development: Hilary Poole
Designer: Annemarie Redmond
Copyeditor: Peter Jaskowiak
Editorial Assistant: Leigh Eron

Series ISBN: 978-1-4222-3721-2
Hardback ISBN: 978-1-4222-3727-4
E-Book ISBN: 978-1-4222-8060-7

Library of Congress Cataloging-in-Publication Data
Names: Poole, Hilary W., author.
Title: Nighttime fears / by H.W. Poole.
Description: Broomall, PA : Mason Crest, [2018] | Series: Childhood fears and
   anxieties | Audience: Age 12+ | Audience: Grade 7 to 8. | Includes bibliographical
   references and index.
Identifiers: LCCN 2016053127 (print) | LCCN 2017020112 (ebook) | ISBN
   9781422280607 (ebook) | ISBN 9781422237274
Subjects: LCSH: Anxiety in children—Juvenile literature. | Anxiety—Juvenile literature.
Classification: LCC BF723.A5 (ebook) | LCC BF723.A5 P665 2018 (print) | DDC
   155.4/1246—d c23
LC record available at https://lccn.loc.gov/2016053127

Printed and bound in the United States of America.

First printing
9 8 7 6 5 4 3 2 1

TABLE OF CONTENTS

Key Icons to Look for:

Words to Understand: These words with their easy-to-understand definitions will increase the reader's understanding of the text, while building vocabulary skills.

Sidebars: This boxed material within the main text allows readers to build knowledge, gain insights, explore possibilities, and broaden their perspectives by weaving together additional information to provide realistic and holistic perspectives.

Educational Videos: Readers can view videos by scanning our QR codes, which will provide them with additional educational content to supplement the text. Examples include news coverage, moments in history, speeches, iconic sports moments, and much more.

Text-Dependent Questions: These questions send the reader back to the text for more careful attention to the evidence presented there.

Research Projects: Readers are pointed toward areas of further inquiry connected to each chapter. Suggestions are provided for projects that encourage deeper research and analysis.

Series Glossary of Key Terms: This back-of-the-book glossary contains terminology used throughout the series. Words found here increase the reader's ability to read and comprehend higher-level books and articles in this field.

SERIES INTRODUCTION

Who among us does not have memories of an intense childhood fear? Fears and anxieties are a part of *every* childhood. Indeed, these fears are fodder for urban legends and campfire tales alike. And while the details of these legends and tales change over time, they generally have at their base predictable childhood terrors such as darkness, separation from caretakers, or bodily injury.

We know that fear has an evolutionary component. Infants are helpless, and, compared to other mammals, humans have a very long developmental period. Fear ensures that curious children will stay close to caretakers, making them less likely to be exposed to danger. This means that childhood fears are adaptive, making us more likely to survive, and even thrive, as a species.

Unfortunately, there comes a point when fear and anxiety cease to be useful. This is especially problematic today, for there has been a startling increase in anxiety among children and adolescents. In fact, 25 percent of 13- to 18-year-olds now have mild to moderate anxiety, and the *median* age of onset for anxiety disorders is just 11 years old.

Why might this be? Some say that the contemporary United States is a nation preoccupied with risk, and it is certainly possible that our children are absorbing this preoccupation as well. Certainly, our exposure to potential threats has never been greater. We see graphic images via the media and have more immediate news of all forms of disaster. This can lead our children to feel more vulnerable, and it may increase the likelihood that they respond with fear. If children based their fear on the news that they see on Facebook or on TV, they would dramatically overestimate the likelihood of terrible things happening.

As parents or teachers, what do we do about fear? As in other areas of life, we provide our children with guidance and education on a daily basis. We teach them about the signs and feelings of fear. We discuss and normalize typical fear reactions, and support them in tackling difficult situations despite fear. We explain—and demonstrate by example—how to identify "negative thinking traps" and generate positive coping thoughts instead.

But to do so effectively, we might need to challenge some of our own assumptions about fear. Adults often assume that they must protect their children from fear and help them to avoid scary situations, when sometimes the best course is for the child to face the fear and conquer it. This is counterintuitive for many adults: after all, isn't it our job to reassure our children and help them feel better? Yes, of course! Except when it isn't. Sometimes they need us to help them confront their fears and move forward anyway.

That's where these volumes come in. When it comes to fear, balanced information is critical. Learning about fear as it relates to many different areas can help us to help our children remember that although you don't choose whether to be afraid, you do choose how to handle it. These volumes explore the world of childhood fears, seeking to answer important questions: How much is too much? And how can fear be positive, functioning to mobilize us in the face of danger?

Fear gives us the opportunity to step up and respond with courage and resilience. It pushes us to expand our sphere of functioning to areas that might feel unfamiliar or risky. When we are a little nervous or afraid, we tend to prepare a little more, look for more information, ask more questions—and all of this can function to help us expand the boundaries of our lives in a positive direction. So, while fear might *feel* unpleasant, there is no doubt that it can have a positive outcome.

Let's teach our children that.

—Anne Walters, Ph.D.
Chief Psychologist, Emma Pendleton Bradley Hospital
Clinical Associate Professor,
Alpert Medical School of Brown University

Sounds that are no big deal during the day can seem scary at night.

CHAPTER ONE

FEAR OF THE DARK

The most basic nighttime fear is fear of darkness itself. Fear of the dark is both common and ancient. Our earliest ancestors had good reason to fear the nighttime. Many **predators** hunt when the sun is down, hiding in the shadows to snatch up their prey.

In fact, when we talk about our fear of the dark, we aren't even really calling our fear by the right name! It's not darkness that's scary, really—it's the fact that darkness can hide things that *are* scary. You might hear a noise, but you can't see what caused it. You might see a shadow, but you can't tell what's making it. Plus, it is often much quieter at night than it is during the day. That means that sounds are **amplified**—they *seem* even louder than they would when the sun is shining. Again, this all goes back to our ancient ancestors. Evolution has taught us to be on alert when we can't see what's going on.

 **WORDS TO UNDERSTAND**

amplified: made louder.

phobia: extreme fear of a particular thing.

predators: hunters.

pressurized: to put under pressure, meaning some kind of physical force.

Our ancestors had good reason to fear the dark.

WHO GOES THERE?

One fascinating thing about our fear of the dark is that it does not usually appear right away. There are exceptions, of course, but most babies are not afraid of the dark. Generally, children only start to fear the dark when they are between one and two years old. That's probably not an accident; in fact, it's about the same age when young kids begin moving around on their own. If you view it from the perspective of our ancestors, a fear of the dark could be very useful. After all, cave people didn't have cribs or safety gates! A fear of darkness helped keep curious babies from wandering around in the middle of the night, when it was easy for them to either hurt themselves or get eaten.

Fear of the dark tends to be the worst in kids who are between two and six years old. The preschool years are when our imaginations are really fired up. Kids under six can't always tell what's real and what isn't. That means they are more likely to believe in scary things like monsters and ghosts. It also means that if they hear a noise, kids can easily imagine a whole list of terrifying things that the sound could be. Night-lights can help, as can security objects like stuffed animals or favorite blankets. Families also can do a lot to reassure their younger members—see chapter four for more on this.

GROWING OUT OF IT . . . OR NOT

As kids get older, they learn that there is definitely no monster under the bed. By the time kids are starting school, most are no longer super scared of

Some adults are afraid of the dark, but they often fear burglars rather than monsters.

the dark. A small night-light might be all they need to feel secure.

However, just because many kids outgrow being afraid of the dark, that does not mean everybody does! As we become more aware of the real world, we also become more aware that bad things do happen. So the dark might still scare you because you think, "Sure, I know there's

WHAT IS THUNDER?

One thing that scares a lot of kids, at night especially, is a loud thunderstorm. But sometimes if you understand what causes something, then the thing itself is no longer so scary. So, what's thunder?

This might sound strange, but thunder is actually caused by lightning. During a storm, clouds build up huge amounts of static electricity, which is eventually released as lightning. You may not see it, because sometimes lightning bolts jump from one cloud to another, rather than from a cloud to the ground. But either way, lightning heats up the air around it very quickly—the air around a bolt of lightning can get to almost 50,000 degrees Fahrenheit (more than 27,000 degrees Celsius). It is also more highly **pressurized** than regular air—there's as much as 100 times more pressure.

This all happens very quickly, and that speed causes the compressed air to suddenly explode outward, away from the lightning. This creates a shock wave of air pressure, which reaches our ears as thunder. Because light travels through air faster than sound does, we see the lightning before we hear the thunder.

It's possible to estimate how far away the storm is by counting the time between the thunder and the lightning. Each second that passes between no monster in the house . . . but there could be a burglar!"

The truth is, it can be hard sometimes for people of any age to feel safe at night. Recent research has found that some adults remain afraid of the dark, even long after they no longer believe in monsters. Of course, adults might not admit that they are afraid; they might sleep with

EDUCATIONAL VIDEO

Check out this video about thunder.

the two is equal to roughly 1,000 feet (300 meters). So, for example, if you see lightning and then count the seconds, and you get to 5 before you hear the thunder, that means the storm is about 5,000 feet away, or just under 1 mile.

You hear thunder and see lightning at different times because light and sound travel at different speeds.

People of all ages use night-lights to help them feel secure in the dark.

the television on but not confess the real reason why. After all, fearing the dark sounds like a "kid problem," not a grown-up problem. But, as we discussed, fear of darkness is actually wired into

the human brain; so it's actually not surprising that some people never quite "get over it." Fortunately, there are lots of strategies that may help bedtime be more restful and less frightening—this will be covered in chapter four.

A small number of people become so afraid that they are said to have a **phobia**. Phobias are extreme fears of particular things. Extreme fear of the dark has a few different names: *nyctophobia, achluophobia,* or *scotophobia.* Whatever you call it, people with this phobia often imagine terrifying scenarios, sort of like scenes from horror movies, the minute the lights go out. They might suffer from panic attacks, which involve dizziness, trouble breathing, sweating, and feeling extremely upset. People whose fear of the dark is this extreme may need medical help to handle it. (For more information, see the book *Phobias* in this set.)

RESEARCH PROJECT

Find out more about phobias. Research one that is most interesting to you. Find out the possible causes of the phobia—for example, many people with cynophobia, an extreme fear of dogs, had a bad interaction with a dog when they were children. Also find out what can be done to overcome the phobia, and create a pamphlet with advice for people who have the problem.

TEXT-DEPENDENT QUESTIONS

1. At what age does fear of the dark begin? Why?

2. Why might fear of the dark be beneficial?

3. What are names for an extreme fear of the dark?

Some people are not afraid of what's outside but rather what is inside their own dreams.

CHAPTER TWO

DREAMS AND NIGHTMARES

Fear of the dark is really fear of whatever is lurking in the dark. In other words, it's a fear of things that are outside yourself. But that's not the only type of nighttime fear. In fact, it's not even the worst one. Far scarier for most people is not what's outside, but what's lurking inside in our dreams.

WHAT ARE DREAMS?

Some people remember a great many of their dreams, while other people remember very few. Whether we can remember or not, we all dream. In fact, experts believe people usually dream for roughly two hours every night. But what is a dream, exactly?

When people are sleeping, their eyes are closed, they are breathing deeply, and if you speak to them, they usually won't answer. Sometimes people roll over if they get uncomfortable; other people snore or mumble in their sleep. But, overall, if you just look at a sleeping person, it looks like there isn't much going on.

WORDS TO UNDERSTAND

occasional: from time to time; not often.

speculate: to make a guess about something.

subconscious: thoughts and feelings you have but may not be aware of.

surreal: strange; unlike real life.

symbolic: something that stands in for something else.

Meanwhile, a great deal can be happening inside a sleeping person's mind. Scientists have measured electrical activity in the brains of sleeping people, and they also study things like blood flow and oxygen levels. There's a phase of sleep called REM (rapid eye movement) sleep, and during that phase, our brains are extremely active.

During periods of deep sleep, the body becomes essentially paralyzed. Your body does this on purpose. After all, just because you are running in a dream, that doesn't mean you want to be running in your sleep! But even though our bodies are still, our minds are thinking, feeling, and telling stories. We are dreaming.

Although you might dream about running or flying, your brain usually prevents you from trying to actually do these things.

WHY DO WE DREAM?

Have you ever tried to explain a dream to someone? Most likely, images and feelings that felt so vivid at the time suddenly made no sense when you tried to express them in words. That raises an interesting question. Why do our brains bother with dreams? It seems like a lot of work to create these complicated sleep-time "movies" that seem to have no use during the day.

There is no perfect answer to the question of why we dream. But we do know that parts of the brain that control learning and emotions while we are awake are also active during REM sleep. It's possible that we invent dreams in order to make sense of the various signals that are coming from those parts of the brain. Other people have **speculated** that dreams are a way for the brain to "work on" particular concerns or problems. While the body rests, the mind processes the many events of the previous day and prepares itself for whatever is coming tomorrow. One writer called dreams a "rehearsal space" for the brain.

Interestingly, while some dreams are easy to understand, many of them are strange and nonsensical. A part of the brain called the visual cortex is especially active during REM sleep, while the more logical parts of our brains are less active. That may be why so many dreams involve **surreal** images that only seem to make sense while you are asleep.

EDUCATIONAL VIDEO

For more information on dreams and nightmares, check out this video!

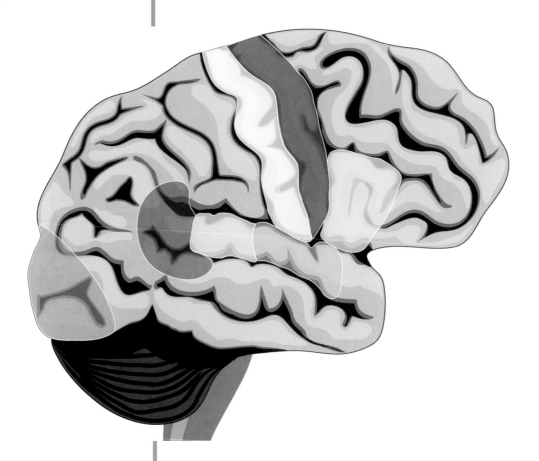

The visual cortex (colored pink in this illustration) remains active while we sleep.

How the content of dreams connects to real life isn't always clear. Lots of people have tried to figure it out, though. Famous analysts like Sigmund Freud and Carl Jung (see box) have written about the **symbolic** value of dreams. For example, some people believe that dreaming about flying is a reflection of the person's self-confidence. In this interpretation, people who fly high over buildings are confident, while people who fly close to the ground are feeling frustrated or helpless in some way.

Another common dream involves being forced to take a test and not knowing any of the answers.

FREUD AND JUNG

Sigmund Freud (1856–1939) was a psychoanalyst whose work had a huge influence on how we think about the human mind. He believed that dreams are expressions of **subconscious** wishes, many of which we would not (and maybe should not) express in real life. He often worked with his patients to interpret their dreams, as a way of understanding what was really going on that the patients could not or would not say.

Initially a student of Freud, the analyst Carl Jung (1875–1961) ended up breaking away from his teacher. Jung came to believe that dreams were not just a reflection of individual wishes, or what he called the "personal unconscious." He believed that dreams also connect to a broader realm that is shared among all humans. Jung called this our "collective unconscious." The idea is that there are certain images and concepts that we all understand. Jung believed we inherit this understanding from our ancestors. So while Freud looked at dreams as highly individual experiences that are unique to a single person, Jung emphasized the ways in which all dreamers are connected by virtue of being human.

Sigmund Freud

Carl Jung

Some people say this dream has to do with feeling exposed, while others think it refers to a "lesson" that we still need to learn. It's also common for people to dream about death, either their own or someone else's. But people who analyze dreams are pretty sure that death in a dream does not refer to actual death. Instead, they think that dreaming about death is a symbolic reference to any big change or transformation in the dreamer's life.

It's important to remember that there is no official meaning for any given dream. People have theories about what the different symbols in dreams might mean, but they are just theories. Dreams are very personal. A flying dream may mean one thing

People of all ages have nightmares, but they are most common among kids between three and six years old.

to you, but it might have a different meaning to someone else.

WHEN DREAMS GO BAD

Frightening dreams are called nightmares. Nightmares usually wake us up, and we'll often, though not always, remember what happened in the dream. Nightmares tend to happen very late at night, when the person has been asleep for some time. (This is part of what distinguishes them from night terrors, which are discussed in chapter three.) People of all ages have nightmares from time to time, but they are most common in kids under the age of 10. Very young kids can be especially

One very common nightmare is where you suddenly have to take a test you haven't studied for.

RESEARCH PROJECT

Interview people of different ages about their dreams. Ask questions like: *Do you remember your dreams? What kinds of things do you dream about? Is there a specific dream that's important to you that you're willing to share?* Then, if you like to write, turn some of the most interesting dreams into short stories. If you prefer visual art, make pictures to capture the surreal images people described to you. And if you are more of a numbers person, try to group the dreams into different categories, such as chasing dreams, test-taking dreams, and so on. Do you see any patterns in the types of dreams people have?

bothered by nightmares, because as we noted in chapter one, they aren't always able to tell what's real and what isn't.

Just as we don't know exactly why we dream, we don't know exactly why we have nightmares. Sometimes there is a clear relationship between stressful events during the day and nightmares at night, but sometimes the link isn't so obvious. When someone has been through a serious trauma, he or she might have nightmares for some time afterward. Interestingly, while some nightmares include "replaying" the traumatic event, frequently there is no direct connection between the trauma and the dream.

Most kids have **occasional** nightmares between the ages of three and six, and nightmares may continue off-and-on all the way to adulthood. But while it's common to have nightmares sometimes, it is rare to have them frequently: fewer than 4 percent of parents say that their young child has nightmares "often." As long as nightmares only happen every once in a while, doctors do not think there is any reason to worry about them.

But if you have nightmares regularly and they start to bother you, it is a good idea to talk to a trusted adult, such as a parent, doctor, or teacher. Maybe something is going on in your life that is causing you a lot of stress. You may need help working on that problem, so that you can get the sleep you need. A very small number of people have a problem called nightmare disorder (see chapter four), which is when frequent nightmares cause problems and distress during the day.

There are a few things we can all do to try and reduce the chances of having a nightmare. Avoiding scary stories or TV shows before bed is one good suggestion—that way, you will not have frightening images in your mind as you try to fall asleep. Having a night-light can be helpful; if you wake up from a bad dream, you can easily remind yourself that you are safe in your own bed. Finally, even if you think you are too old for this, there's no shame in having a security item such as a stuffed animal or blanket, that helps you feel comforted when you wake up from a bad dream. See chapter four for other tips about getting more restful sleep.

 TEXT-DEPENDENT QUESTIONS

1. What are some possible reasons why we dream?

2. At what ages do we start having nightmares?

3. What are some possible causes of nightmares?

A person having a night terror may scream and cry out, even though he or she is still asleep and probably won't remember anything the next morning.

CHAPTER THREE

NIGHT TERRORS

Night terrors (also called "sleep terrors") are much more **dramatic** than regular nightmares. Someone having a night terror may scream, thrash around in bed, and act extremely scared—all without waking up. The person usually doesn't remember what happened the next day, either. In a sense, night terrors are just as scary for the rest of the family as they are for the person having them. But the good news is that night terrors, like nightmares, are totally normal and will usually **resolve** themselves in time.

CAUSES OF NIGHT TERRORS

Night terrors are most common in kids between the ages of 4 and 12, although older people may get them, too. They tend to occur in an earlier phase of sleep than nightmares do, which means they often happen earlier at night. An adult who

WORDS TO UNDERSTAND

console: to make an upset person feel better.

dramatic: intense and vivid.

migraine: a very bad headache.

resolve: work out; conclude.

Opposite: The cause of night terrors may not be completely clear.

has had a night terror may remember parts of it later, but a child almost never will. People having night terrors stay asleep the whole time—even if their eyes are open!

The cause of night terrors can vary from person to person, and it may never be entirely clear. We do know that being extremely tired can help bring on a night terror, as can fevers and sleeping in strange places. Night terrors might have some connection to anxiety or stress during the day. Other times, the causes are physical: things like migraines and head injuries can bring

NIGHTMARES VERSUS NIGHT TERRORS

Nightmares	Night terrors
They usually occur late at night, after the dreamer has been asleep for some time.	They usually occur earlier, soon after going to sleep.
They often cause the dreamer to wake up.	The dreamer usually does not wake up.
The dreamer usually remembers the dream (at least at first).	The dreamer usually has no memory of the event at all.
The dreamer usually understands that he or she has had a nightmare.	The dreamer is often confused and not sure what just happened.

EDUCATIONAL VIDEO

Scan this code for a video about the difference between nightmares and night terrors.

on night terrors, and certain medications can, too. Finally, night terrors do tend to run in families, so that if a parent had night terrors as a child, their kids might also have them.

COPING WITH NIGHT TERRORS

Because people don't wake up while they are having night terrors, it's very difficult to **console** them. Unfortunately, the most that family members can usually do is wait for the night terror to pass. One important thing is to make sure that people having night terrors are in a safe spot, so that they don't fall or hurt themselves accidentally.

Although night terrors are no fun at all, they usually are not a big problem. Of course, it can be somewhat embarrassing to come downstairs for breakfast and find out that you woke up your family in the middle of the night! But as long as the person having night terrors is safe in bed, some teasing from your brothers and sisters is usually the worst of it. Kids tend to outgrow night terrors by middle school.

However, if night terrors continue every night, or if you find that you are tired all the time because of them, you might need to talk about it with a doctor. One important first step is create a sleep diary. A sleep diary is a record of when a person goes to sleep, how well she sleeps, and

when she wakes up. And, in this case, it should also note every time the person has a sleep terror. Obviously, this is something the person having the problem can't do alone, so a parent or other family member needs to take charge of making notes. These notes will be important when you talk to a

Night terrors usually go away by themselves, but your health-care provider can give you advice about how to handle them in the meantime.

RESEARCH
PROJECT

Even if you don't have
a problem, keep a
sleep diary for one
week. The National
Sleep Foundation has
a sample diary on their
website, at https://
sleepfoundation.
org/sleep-diary/
SleepDiaryv6.pdf.
There are also sleep
diary apps that you
can use on a phone or
tablet. At the end of the
week, write up a report
on your sleep habits.
Do you notice any
relationship between
what you did right
before you went to bed
and how you slept?

doctor, since a sleep diary can reveal patterns in
when and how well you sleep.

If the doctor agrees that the night terrors are
a problem, you may undergo what's called a sleep
study. These take place in special places called
sleep labs, where people can spend the night
and have their sleep monitored. The information

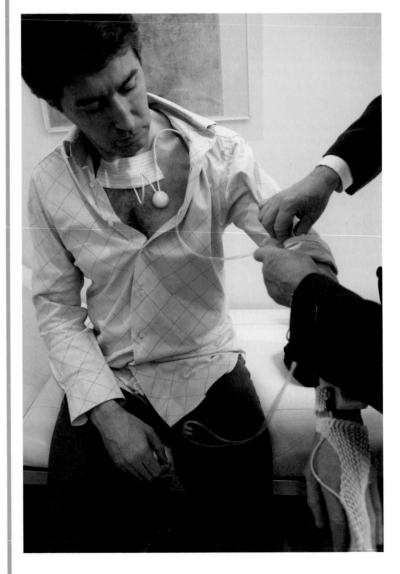

**If night terrors
are creating big
problems, you
might undergo a
sleep study.**

gathered from the sleep study helps doctors determine what the problem is and figure out how to treat it.

If there is a physical problem that's causing the sleep terrors, your doctor can address that. If a lot of daytime stress is the culprit, a doctor might be able to suggest some strategies that can help with relaxation. And because sleep terrors can actually be caused by not sleeping *enough*, improving sleep habits can make a big difference. If nothing else helps, there are medications that can be prescribed. However, this is almost never done for children, due to the risks and potential side effects of the medication.

 TEXT-DEPENDENT QUESTIONS

1. What are night terrors?

2. How are night terrors different from nightmares?

3. What is a sleep study?

It's important that your bed is a place where you feel comfortable and safe.

CHAPTER FOUR

CONQUERING THE DARK

Whether it's fear of the dark, nightmares, or night terrors, nighttime fears can be really unpleasant experiences. But as we've discussed, feeling anxious at nighttime is totally normal. Overall, the vast majority of nighttime fears can be eased with something called good sleep **hygiene**.

WHAT IS SLEEP HYGIENE

When we talk about hygiene, we are usually referring to personal cleanliness—things like taking regular showers or washing our hands after we use the bathroom. Sleep hygiene, however, refers to the habits that help us get better sleep. Remember what we said earlier: nighttime fears can be made worse by lack of sleep. So the better your sleep hygiene, the less you'll have to fear.

One part of sleep hygiene is the condition of your bedroom. If you are afraid of the dark, you probably don't want piles of stuff lying around. For example,

WORDS TO UNDERSTAND

hygiene: habits that increase health or cleanliness.

melatonin: a substance that helps the body regulate sleep.

stimulant: a group of substances that speed up bodily processes.

By day, this is just a messy room—but at night, the piles of stuff can cast weird shadows.

what looks like a pile of clothes during the day could make you nervous at night, particularly if you start wondering what might be hiding underneath it. If you can, remove any objects that cast weird shadows when the lights are low.

Try to avoid both TV and computer or tablet screens right before you go to bed. And definitely don't bring them to bed with you. First of all, it's too tempting to play on a phone or tablet when you should be sleeping—even adults find their phones hard to resist! It might seem like having the TV on is good for fighting fears, but all it really does is keep you awake. That can leave you overtired, which can make the fears and nightmares much worse.

Be honest: Have you ever stayed up later than you intended because you were using a phone or tablet? Lots of people have. Turns out, it wasn't just the excitement of the device keeping us awake. Electronic devices emit "blue light," which has been shown to make it harder for people to fall asleep. The light blocks activity of the pineal gland, which releases **melatonin**. Melatonin helps let the brain know that it's time to rest. So if you are blocking melatonin, you are keeping yourself awake. Many devices now have settings that limit or eliminate the blue light, which can help make them less distracting. There's also a special type of sunglasses called blocking glasses, which block the blue light from other people's devices.

Another thing that can keep you awake is caffeine. Caffeine is a substance found in coffee, tea,

The blue light from phones, tablets, and computers can interfere with sleep.

EDUCATIONAL VIDEO

Here's a video with more advice about sleep hygiene.

many sodas, and even chocolate. It is a **stimulant**, meaning that it speeds up bodily functions. It can take hours for caffeine to pass through the body, so you should be cautious about consuming products with caffeine close to bedtime.

Scary TV shows, movies, games, and books might also cause anxiety at night. Horror stories can be fun sometimes, but they can also keep us awake. Plus, they put alarming images in our heads that can come back to haunt us while we are lying in the dark trying to sleep.

PARENTS AND DOCTORS

Everybody is different, and when it comes to fear, not every coping strategy works. In fact, not everyone agrees on the best way to go about it.

For example, as we discussed earlier, many young kids are afraid to go to bed because they fear there may be a monster under the bed or in the closet. Trying to be helpful, many parents come up with ways to "defeat" the monster. For instance, some parents put water in a spray bottle and label it "anti-monster spray." They then encourage the child to spray under the bed, around the closet, or whatever spot the child is worried about. Others create bedtime rituals where they pretend to defeat the monsters or chase them away.

Although parents mean well, a lot of experts don't agree that these are great ideas. After all,

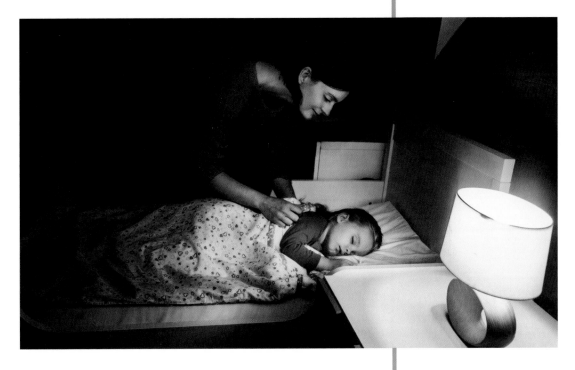

if you suspect that you have a monster under your bed, and your parents give you some kind of weapon to fight off the monster, that pretty much confirms that the monster is really there! These anti-monster rituals can sometimes extend the amount of time kids are afraid.

Many doctors prefer that families take a different approach. They certainly should not make fun of kids or say something like, "Don't be silly, monsters don't exist!" But they could say, "I understand why you might be worried about a monster. But let's go look in your closet together, and you'll see that there is nothing to be afraid of." In other words, experts say the best strategy has two parts: one, be sympathetic about the fear, but, two, do not agree that it is correct.

Knowing that someone is coming to check on them helps many kids sleep more peacefully.

Another strategy would be for a parent to say, "I will come check on you every X number of minutes, to make sure you are okay." Then the parent would come back regularly—maybe first every 2 minutes, then every 5 minutes, then 10 . . . and so on until the child falls asleep. That way, kids are reassured they are not alone, but they get to enjoy the "victory" of being able to fall asleep on their own. In time, kids will learn that their bedrooms are safe places, and that they can succeed in falling asleep.

Reading is a great way to transition from a busy day to a restful sleep.

LEARNING TO RELAX

But maybe it's not monsters or murderers that keep you up. Maybe it's stress at home or at school.

NIGHTMARE DISORDER

Whether it's nightmares, terrors, or basic fear of the dark, the vast majority of nighttime fears can be resolved with patience and good sleep hygiene. But every once in a while, sleep problems crop up that are more serious. As a group, these problems are called *parasomnias*. Parasomnias include recurring night terrors and nightmare disorder.

People who have nightmare disorder experience long, very scary nightmares on a regular basis. These nightmares damage the person's ability to get a good night's sleep, which leads to problems with work or school. Nightmare disorder can be mild (less than once a week), moderate (at least once a week), or severe (every night). There is no obvious cause of nightmare disorder. Scientific studies of twins have shown that genetics are likely a factor—in other words, nightmare disorder tends to run in families.

Unfortunately, these kinds of "scares" are a lot harder to avoid than horror movies. It's not possible to rid ourselves of all stress. And, ironically, the more you think about the fact that you are stressed, the worse it's going to get! Keep in mind that all people worry sometimes, and that all people have trouble falling asleep sometimes. (For more on how humans are born worriers, see the volume *Anxiety and Fear in Daily Life* in this set.) Instead of being critical of yourself, try some of these strategies to help yourself wind down at the end of the day:

- **Chill out.** If you simply go up to bed and shut the light off without any transition, it can be hard to let go of the day. Instead, think of

Sometimes having a buddy around can make sleep less scary.

the hour or so before you try to fall asleep as your time to relax. Try listening to music, taking a warm bath or shower, cuddling with your favorite pet . . . whatever helps you feel more peaceful. Some people love to read, others meditate for a few minutes before bed. It's not always possible to get a lot of quiet time before bed, so forgive yourself if it doesn't work out every night. But as much as you can, try to begin winding down from your day a little earlier.

- **Reassure yourself.** You need to feel like your room and bed are safe places. If you associate your bedroom with fear and nightmares, it can be hard to relax when you are there. Sometimes it can help to spend time lying in bed when you are not actually trying to sleep. Maybe invite your parent, sibling, or favorite pet into your room to just "hang out" for a while. Having good associations with your bedroom may help you feel more comfortable later.

- **A little at a time.** If you are struggling with a fear of the dark, try conquering it in small steps. For instance, maybe sleep with a bedside light on for a week. Then turn that light out and sleep with the hallway light plus a night-light. After a week of that, maybe try closing the door and going to sleep with just the night-light.

Keep in mind that there is no medal given out for "perfect" sleeping! The only goal is to find what works for *you*. Each night is another chance to take one more small step toward that goal.

RESEARCH PROJECT

Make a poster or pamphlet about sleep hygiene. You can gather advice from this chapter, but also use the Further Reading titles and your own research to find additional suggestions about how to sleep better.

TEXT-DEPENDENT QUESTIONS

1. Why does screen time interfere with sleep?

2. What approach do some parents take to their children's bedtime time fears that doctors wish they wouldn't? Why?

3. What is nightmare disorder?

FURTHER READING

Alter, Robyn, and Crystal Clarke. *The Anxiety Workbook for Kids.* Oakland, CA: Instant Help, 2016.

Cuthbert, Timothy, and Rebecca Kajander. *Be the Boss of Your Sleep.* Minneapolis, MN: Free Spirit Publishing, 2007.

MacMillan, Amanda. "Sleep Tips for Kids of All Ages." WebMD. http://www. webmd.com/parenting/raising-fit-kids/recharge/kids-sleep-tips.

Mayo Clinic. "Sleep Terrors (Night Terrors)." http://www.mayoclinic.org/ diseases-conditions/night-terrors/basics/definition/con-20032552.

National Sleep Foundation. "Children and Bedtime: Fears and Nightmares." https://sleepfoundation.org/ask-the-expert/ children-and-bedtime-fears-and-nightmares.

Poole, H. W. *Sleep Disorders*. Broomall, PA: Mason Crest, 2016.

WikiHow. "How to Not Be Afraid of the Dark." http://www.wikihow.com/ Not-Be-Afraid-of-the-Dark.

EDUCATIONAL VIDEOS

Chapter One: TestTube 101. "What Causes Thunder?" https://youtu.be/ EGyubhH13V4.

Chapter Two: DNews. "Why Do We Get Nightmares?" https://youtu.be/ iKgbdUmZnnM.

Chapter Three: Intermountain Moms. "What's the Difference between Nightmares and Night Terrors?" https://youtu.be/ds8GRH4xmN8.

Chapter Four: Watchwellcast. "How to Sleep Better." https://youtu.be/ 3eLfn7Ewx_s.

SERIES GLOSSARY

adaptive: a helpful response to a particular situation.

bias: a feeling against a particular thing or idea.

biofeedback: monitoring of bodily functions with the goal of learning to control those functions.

cognitive: relating to the brain and thought.

comorbid: when one illness or disorder is present alongside another one.

context: the larger situation in which an event takes place.

diagnose: to identify an illness or disorder.

exposure: having contact with something.

extrovert: a person who enjoys being with others.

harassment: picking on another person frequently and deliberately.

hypnosis: creating a state of consciousness where someone is awake but highly open to suggestion.

inhibitions: feelings that restricts what we do or say.

introvert: a person who prefers being alone.

irrational: baseless; something that's not connected to reality.

melatonin: a substance that helps the body regulate sleep.

milestone: an event that marks a stage in development.

motivating: something that makes you want to work harder.

occasional: from time to time; not often.

panic attack: sudden episode of intense, overwhelming fear.

paralyzing: something that makes you unable to move (can refer to physical movement as well as emotions).

peers: people who are roughly the same age as you.

perception: what we see and believe to be true.

persistent: continuing for a noticeable period.

phobia: extreme fear of a particular thing.

preventive: keeping something from happening.

probability: the likelihood that a particular thing will happen.

psychological: having to do with the mind and thoughts.

rational: based on a calm understanding of facts, rather than emotion.

sedative: a type of drug that slows down bodily processes, making people feel relaxed or even sleepy.

self-conscious: overly aware of yourself, to the point that it makes you awkward.

serotonin: a chemical in the brain that is important in moods.

stereotype: an oversimplified idea about a type of person that may not be true for any given individual.

stigma: a sense of shame or disgrace associated with a particular state of being.

stimulant: a group of substances that speed up bodily processes.

subconscious: thoughts and feelings you have but may not be aware of.

syndrome: a condition.

treatable: describes a medical condition that can be healed.

upheaval: a period of great change or uncertainty.

INDEX

ABOUT THE ADVISOR

Anne S. Walters is Clinical Associate Professor of Psychiatry and Human Behavior at the Alpert Medical School of Brown University. She is also Chief Psychologist for Bradley Hospital. She is actively involved in teaching activities within the Clinical Psychology Training Programs of the Alpert Medical School and serves as Child Track Seminar Co-Coordinator. Dr. Walters completed her undergraduate work at Duke University, graduate school at Georgia State University, internship at UTexas Health Science Center, and postdoctoral fellowship at Brown University.

ABOUT THE AUTHOR

H. W. Poole is a writer and editor of books for young people, including the sets, *Families Today* and *Mental Illnesses and Disorders: Awareness and Understanding* (Mason Crest). She created the *Horrors of History* series (Charlesbridge) and the *Ecosystems* series (Facts On File). She has also been responsible for many critically acclaimed reference books, including *Political Handbook of the World* (CQ Press) and the *Encyclopedia of Terrorism* (SAGE). She was coauthor and editor of *The History of the Internet* (ABC-CLIO), which won the 2000 American Library Association RUSA award.

PHOTO CREDITS